The Jewel Princesses and the Missing Crown

READ MORE BOOKS ABOUT

THE JEWEL KINGDOM

1 The Ruby Princess Runs Away

2 The Sapphire Princess Meets a Monster

3 The Emerald Princess Plays a Trick

4 The Diamond Princess Saves the Day

5 The Ruby Princess Sees a Ghost

6 The Sapphire Princess Hunts for Treasure

7 The Emerald Princess Finds a Fairy

8 The Diamond Princess and the Little Wizard

Super Special 1: The Jewel Princesses and the Missing Crown

THE JEWEL KINGDOM

The Jewel Princesses and the Missing Crown

JAHNNA N. MALCOLM

Illustrations by Neal McPheeters

SCHOLASTIC INC.
NEW YORK TORONTO LONDON AUCKLAND SYDNEY

ISBN 0-590-37705-1

12 11 10 9 8 7 6 5 4 3 8 9/9 0 1 2 3/0

Printed in the U.S.A.
First Scholastic printing, August 1998

Designed by Elizabeth B. Parisi

To

Bethany Buck

and

Kate Egan

for their amazing Jewel Power!

CONTENTS

The Jewel Princesses and the Missing Crown

The Jewel Kingdom

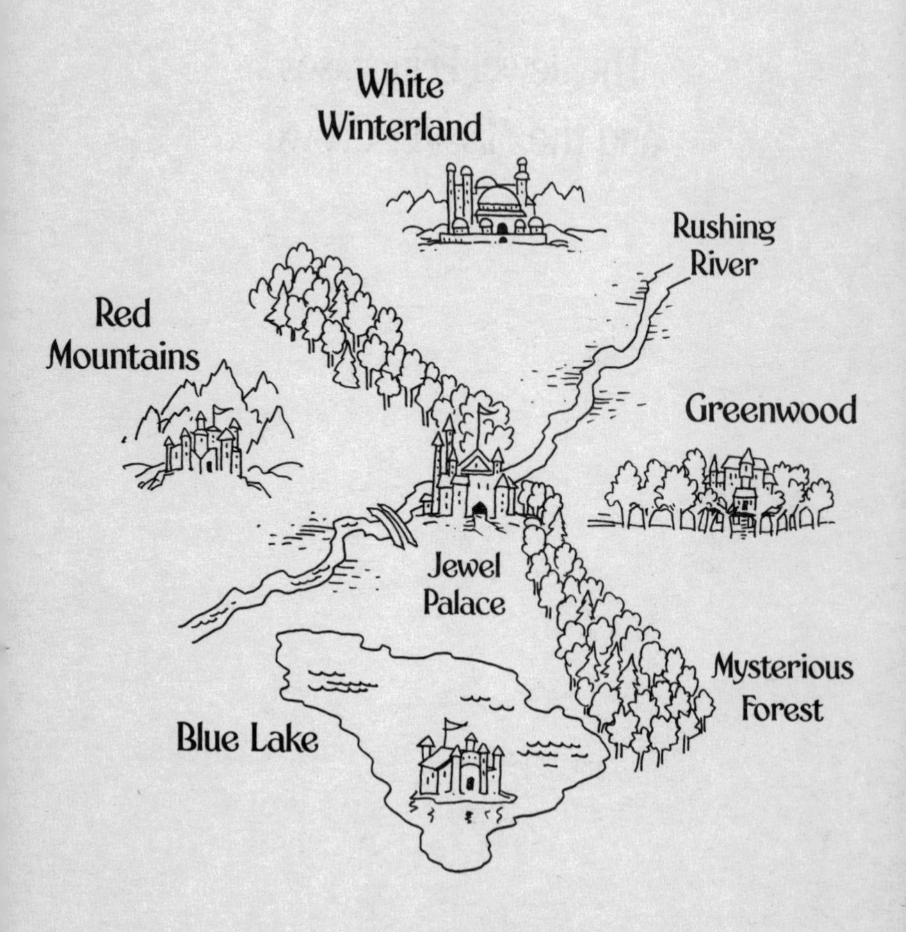

Trouble at the Palace

The sun was rising in the Jewel Kingdom. High above the treetops, a girl in a red velvet dress flew on the back of a great green Dragon.

"Can't you fly any faster, Hapgood?" she called.

"I'm flying as fast as I can, Princess," the Dragon said in his deep voice. "We should reach the Jewel Palace in a few minutes."

A messenger had brought the Ruby Princess an urgent note from the Jewel Palace. *Roxanne, come quickly*, it read. *Your help is needed.*

Princess Roxanne loved adventure, but this seemed serious. Luckily, the Jewel Palace, where her parents lived, was only a short journey from her home in the Red Mountains.

"Hapgood, look!" Roxanne pointed to the road below them. "There's my sister Emily. She must have been sent a message, too."

Emily, the Emerald Princess, was dressed all in green. She was riding Arden, her white unicorn. Emily's bright red hair flew out behind her as she galloped up the road. Emily was a fun-loving princess, but today she looked worried.

The Dragon flew low, preparing to land. "I see the Diamond and Sapphire Princesses waiting at the palace gates," Hapgood called to Roxanne.

"Yes, all of my sisters are here," Roxanne said.

Demetra, the Diamond Princess, was dressed in a white gown. She paced impatiently in front of the gate. Every time she turned, her long brown braid whipped out behind her.

Demetra spotted Roxanne and waved.

Sabrina, the Sapphire Princess, waved, too. She was the gentlest princess. She sat calmly on a rock while Demetra paced. Sabrina's silky blond hair shone in the morning sun. Her pale blue eyes matched the color of her gown.

"Thanks for the ride, Happy," Roxanne said as the Dragon landed on a grassy spot across the road. "Are you sure you can take care of my land without me?"

"I think I can manage," the Dragon chuckled. The great beast flapped his wings and rose into the air. "Good luck, Princess."

"Thanks, Hapgood. I hope I don't need it." Roxanne waved as her friend flew out of sight. Then she hurried across the road to Sabrina and Demetra just as Emily arrived.

"Why are you two waiting out here?" Roxanne asked Sabrina and Demetra.

"We rang the bell on the gate, but there was no answer," Demetra replied.

"No one seems to be home," Sabrina added.

"Then who sent for us?" Emily wondered.

"Me," a tiny voice replied from behind the palace gate. "I'm sorry. So very sorry."

It was Twitter, the royal secretary. The small red bird looked terrible. He was shaking, and some of the feathers from his rainbow plume had fallen out.

"I am sorry you had to wait," Twitter said as he unlocked the gate. "But I'm all by myself."

"Where are Mother and Father?" Sabrina asked.

"Queen Jemma, King Regal, and practically everyone in the palace left a day ago to visit the Sandy Lands," Twitter explained. "They left me in charge, which was a big mistake."

Twitter was very upset. The four princesses looked worried but said nothing.

Twitter held the gate open. "Come inside, all of you. Quickly, please."

The princesses hurried into the courtyard, and Twitter slammed the gate shut.

"Twitter, you must tell us what's wrong," Roxanne said.

The little red bird covered his beak with his wings. "I want to, but I'm so ashamed."

Sabrina touched his rainbow plume. "Take a deep breath, and start from the beginning."

Twitter began slowly. "Last night, I was making my rounds to make sure all was well at the Jewel Palace."

Sabrina smiled at the small red bird. "And?"

"I spotted someone crossing the courtyard."

"Who was it?" Roxanne asked.

"I thought it was one of you," Twitter explained. "She was a young lady, and she wore a dark dress and a cape."

"What did you do?" Emily asked.

Twitter explained that he followed her into the tower. As he flew up the stairs, he called each of the princesses' names. But the girl didn't answer or even turn around.

"That's odd," Demetra said.

"Very odd," Twitter agreed. "And when I reached the tower room, no one was there. I was starting to think my eyes were playing tricks on me, when someone, or something, blew out my lamp."

"Did you light the lamp again?" Roxanne asked.

"Yes, but when I did . . ." Twitter stopped. "Oh, it's too awful to tell."

"Just say it," Roxanne ordered.

Twitter squeezed his eyes closed and cried, "The Great Jeweled Crown was gone!"

The Crown Is Missing!

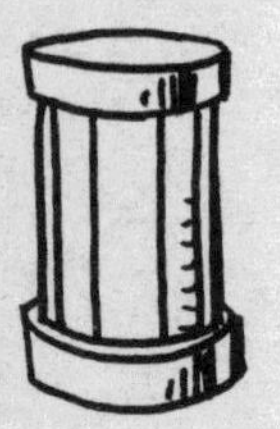

"The Great Jeweled Crown!" Princess Roxanne gasped.

The princesses were quiet as they thought about what that meant.

The crown had been missing once before. It was a terrible time. Lord Bleak and the Darklings ruled. The sun never shone, and no one ever smiled in the Jewel Kingdom.

Luckily, those times were gone. Queen Jemma and King Regal defeated Lord Bleak and took back the crown. Lord Bleak was sent far away across the Black Sea. And Roxanne, Demetra, Emily, and Sabrina were crowned Jewel Princesses.

"My ruby came from the Great Jeweled Crown," Roxanne whispered.

"And my sapphire," Sabrina said.

"And my emerald," Emily added.

"And my diamond," Demetra said.

The princesses knew that whoever had the Great Jeweled Crown had all the power in the kingdom. But now the crown was missing. It was the most terrible thing that could happen.

"We have to send a message to Mother and Father," Sabrina said. "They need to know about this."

Roxanne shook her head. "There isn't

time. It's a whole day's ride to the Sandy Lands."

"Well, what should we do?" Emily asked.

"Go get the crown ourselves," Roxanne replied.

"Us?" Demetra gasped. "But how?"

Roxanne stamped her foot. "We're princesses. We'll find a way."

"I don't know," Demetra said with a frown. "This is very serious."

Sabrina patted Demetra's hand. "It's okay if you are afraid, Demetra. I am, too."

"You know," Emily said, thoughtfully, "we can find the crown if we just follow the clues." Emily loved to solve puzzles.

"Clues?" Demetra repeated.

Emily shrugged. "We know that Twitter saw a girl in a cape go into the tower. And we know it wasn't one of us."

Sabrina nodded. "And it probably wasn't anyone from the Jewel Palace. Everyone went with Mother and Father."

"Let's go to the tower and look around," Demetra said.

"Good idea." Roxanne was already running across the courtyard.

Twitter and the others followed Roxanne up the winding stairs.

In the tower was a round room lined with sparkling windows. At the room's center stood a marble pillar with a velvet pillow on top.

Princess Roxanne stepped up to the pillar and shivered. "There's power in the air. Can you feel it?"

"It's from the crown." The Sapphire Princess pointed to the empty pillow. "This is where the crown is supposed to sit."

The tower was a very special place. It was built by the Great Wizard Gallivant himself. There was more magic in the tower room than anywhere else in the Jewel Kingdom.

A little cry came from Twitter. "I can't believe the crown is missing. It's all my fault!"

"Don't worry, Twitter," Sabrina whispered. "We'll get that crown back."

Demetra suddenly had an idea. "I know!" she cried. "We'll ask my magic mirror to show us the crown."

The Diamond Princess touched the little gold mirror she always wore at her waist. Its magic gave her the power to see people and things in other places.

"Hurry!" Roxanne urged. "We haven't a moment to lose."

Princess Demetra turned away from

her sisters and raised the magic mirror into the air. As she did, the diamonds on its handle began to sparkle.

"Magic Mirror, so shiny bright,
Who stole our crown late last night?"

The glass in the mirror changed into a picture. Demetra could see a girl in a black cape running down a wooded path. She held something under her arm.

"There's our thief!" Demetra cried.

They watched the girl leave the path and look behind her.

"Oh, no!" Demetra gasped as she saw the girl's face. "It's Princess Rudgrin!"

Princess Rudgrin

Princess Rudgrin was the daughter of the evil Lord Bleak.

"We've had trouble with Rudgrin before," Roxanne said with a scowl. She was remembering when they were crowned Jewel Princesses.

On that day, Princess Rudgrin pretended to be Roxanne and was almost crowned the Ruby Princess by mistake.

Later, Rudgrin tried to frighten people away from the Ruby Palace by pretending to be a ghost.

"She's always been trouble," Emily said. "But do you really think she'd try to take over the whole Jewel Kingdom?"

"*She* wouldn't, but her father would," Demetra said.

"Hello!" a voice called from the road below. "Anybody home?"

Twitter nearly jumped out of his feathers. "Oh, dear, oh, dear! I'd better go see who that is."

The royal secretary flew down the stairs. The princesses watched from the window as a horse and rider galloped into the courtyard. The rider wore the rainbow colors of the Jewel Palace guards.

"Captain Armoral sent me to warn you," the young guard reported to Twitter.

"Darklings have been spotted at the border."

Emily caught her breath. "Darklings!"

All of them knew the Darklings served Lord Bleak.

"If Darklings are in our kingdom," Sabrina whispered, "Lord Bleak sent them here."

As she spoke, thunder rumbled in the distance.

"We've got to get that crown back *now*!" Roxanne cried. "Come on!"

Emily was usually the first to volunteer. This time she held back. "Maybe we should try to reach Mother and Father."

"There's no time." Roxanne pointed out the window at the dark clouds swirling in the distance. "We have to stop the darkness before it begins. Are you with me?"

Emily swallowed hard. "I'm with you." She took Roxanne's hand. When their fingers touched, her emerald began to glow.

"Something strange is happening," Emily declared.

Suddenly, Princess Roxanne's ruby began to glow, too.

Princess Sabrina joined her sisters and her blue sapphire shone as brightly as their jewels.

"This is amazing," Sabrina cried as the tower began to shake. "There's magic in this room."

"And in our jewels," Roxanne shouted, as she struggled to hold onto her sisters' hands. "Come on, Demetra!"

When the Diamond Princess took her sisters' hands, a rainbow of light swirled all around them. All at once a ghostly picture of the Great Jeweled Crown appeared above their heads.

"Do you see that?" Princess Emily cried. "It's the crown. Our crown!"

Roxanne threw back her head and shouted,

"Jewel magic! Oh, magic in this tower!
Take us to the Great Jeweled Crown.
Please, use your power!"

In a flash of rainbow light, the Jewel Princesses disappeared.

The Three-headed Monster

The Jewel Princesses were suddenly lying on a beach.

"What happened?" Emily asked, rubbing her hip where she'd landed. She peered into the green fog that surrounded them. Sharp black rocks poked through the mist. "Where are we?"

"I'm not sure," Demetra said as she straightened her crown. "One second we were in the tower, and now we're here."

Sabrina slowly sat up. "We held hands, and our jewels began to glow," she said. "Just like when we were crowned."

"Then Roxanne shouted, 'Take us to the Great Jeweled Crown,' " Emily added.

"And we were sent to this rocky beach," Roxanne finished. She scooped up a handful of wet black sand. "It's not a very nice beach."

"The tower must have sent us here," Sabrina murmured. "It *is* a magical room."

Demetra stood up and brushed the black sand off her white velvet dress. "This is all very strange."

"I'll tell you what's strange," Emily said. "That!"

The Emerald Princess pointed at the shore. A giant three-headed sea serpent glared at them through the mist.

"Run!" Demetra cried. "It's a monster!"

Roxanne was about to run when she noticed something odd about the sea serpent. "That monster isn't moving. Look at its eyes. It doesn't even blink. I don't think it's alive."

"Let's take a closer look," Emily said to Roxanne. Together they inched through the rocks toward the monster.

"Careful, you two," Demetra called in a loud whisper. "It could be a trap."

"We can't let them go alone," Sabrina said. She grabbed Demetra's hand and pulled her toward the water.

As Emily and Roxanne drew closer to the serpent, they realized it wasn't a monster at all. It was the carved nose of a wooden boat. The boat was tied to a pier. The ship's name was painted in black-and-red letters on the side.

"The *Sea Shadow*," Emily read out

loud. "I've never heard of a boat with that name."

"I think we're far away from the palace and our lands," Roxanne replied. She pointed to the murky water lapping at the sides of the ship. A dark brown foam bubbled on top of the waves. "Do you think this could be . . . the Black Sea?"

"The Black Sea!" Emily gasped. "Where Lord Bleak lives?"

Suddenly three Darklings in black hooded capes appeared out of the mist. They were dragging two leather trunks.

Roxanne and Emily ducked behind a large rock. Sabrina and Demetra joined them.

The princesses watched the Darklings carry the trunks onto the ship.

Moments later, a girl in a jet-black cape appeared on the ship. She spoke to a large Darkling who barked orders at the Darkling crew.

"There's Princess Rudgrin," Roxanne hissed. "I'd know her anywhere."

"It looks like they're getting ready to sail," Emily whispered. "We can't let her get away. If the tower room brought us here, Rudgrin must have the crown."

"But how can we stop them?" Demetra asked as two more Darklings carried heavy sacks onto the boat. "We're outnumbered."

While her sisters talked, the Sapphire Princess silently tiptoed to the pier. She didn't like to jump into things like Roxanne and Emily. Sabrina liked to find other ways of solving problems.

Sabrina stared at a stack of supplies on the pier. Maybe something in that pile could help them.

"Aha!" she whispered. "I have an idea."

Sabrina signaled for her sisters to join her. When they did, she pointed to a pile of dark clothes in a basket. "Those are capes," she whispered. "Darkling capes."

"So?" Emily whispered back.

Sabrina smiled. "Follow me."

The princesses all raced to the pier. Sabrina grabbed some capes. "Put these on. Quickly."

Roxanne and Emily did as they were told. But Demetra folded her arms across her chest and shook her head.

"Come on," Sabrina pleaded. "The ship is going to sail. The Darklings will see us."

"No!" Demetra was stubborn. "I don't know if this is a good idea."

"I don't either," Sabrina whispered.

"But right now my plan is the only one we've got."

Demetra had to agree. She put the cape over her head.

With Sabrina leading the way, each princess picked up a wooden box and boarded the ship with the other Darklings.

The princesses looked down at the ground. They tried not to say a word. They had to be very careful not to let anyone see their faces.

They were halfway onto the boat when Emily peeked into her box. "What?" she cried. "Somebody stole these banners from my palace in the Greenwood!"

Several Darklings turned to see who had spoken.

"Shhhh!" Sabrina warned. "You'll give us away."

Emily kept quiet, but she wasn't happy.

She wondered what else had been stolen from the Jewel Kingdom.

Once the girls were on board, Sabrina led them to the deck below. There were four cabins on the lower level. They found an unlocked cabin and jumped inside.

Sabrina threw back her hood and cried, "Thank goodness, we made it!"

"Now all we have to do is find the Great Jeweled Crown and run back to shore!" Roxanne declared.

Emily grinned. "That should be easy."

"It should be, but it's not," Demetra said.

"Why?" Sabrina asked.

Demetra pointed out the round cabin window. There was water all around them. "Because we've sailed."

Sailing the Black Sea

The Black Sea was very rough. Huge waves knocked against the sides of the *Sea Shadow* as it rocked back and forth in the water.

"Whee!" Princess Emily cried as she ran from one side of the cabin to the other. "This is fun!"

"It is not!" Roxanne clutched her stomach and moaned. "My stomach feels terrible."

Emily caught hold of the cabin wall as the ship tilted again. "The strong Ruby Princess is seasick?" she exclaimed. "That's impossible."

The ship tipped to the left, and Roxanne groaned, "Be quiet. We have to find the crown."

"You can't find the crown," Demetra said. "You can't even stand up."

Roxanne made a face at Demetra. "Don't tell me *you're* going to find it."

The Diamond Princess tossed her long braid over her shoulder. "Why not? I'm as brave as you are."

"Don't make me laugh," Roxanne said. She tried to stand up, but another wave slapped against the ship. She sat down quickly.

Sabrina touched Roxanne's shoulder. "Look, you don't always have to be the leader. Sometimes you can be the follower."

"You stay with Sabrina until you feel better," Princess Demetra advised. "Emily and I will find the crown."

Roxanne wanted to argue, but she felt too awful.

"Let's go look through every box, bag, and trunk on this ship." Demetra opened the cabin door a crack and peeked into the hall. "It's all clear, come on."

Emily scurried after Demetra.

No one was in the hallway. Emily found some black bags and started to untie them.

Demetra was poking through two wooden crates when a voice stopped her.

"You, there!" a girl called from the cabin across from her.

Demetra spun around. It was Princess Rudgrin.

"Carry this to the ship's hold," Rudgrin ordered, pointing to a small leather trunk at her feet. "And be quick about it."

"Yes, madam," Demetra mumbled, keeping her head low. She tugged on the handle but the trunk wouldn't budge.

"What's the matter with you?" Princess Rudgrin growled. "I told you to lift the trunk!"

"I'll help her," Emily said, running over to her sister.

"That's more like it." Rudgrin climbed the ladder to the top deck and called over her shoulder, "You two take that trunk below and stay with it. Guard it with your lives."

Emily reached for the trunk. Suddenly

Demetra gasped. Princess Emily's emerald was glowing a bright green.

"Let go!" Demetra hissed. "Someone might see you."

But Emily didn't understand. She lifted the trunk higher. Her emerald glowed even brighter. "What?"

At that moment, Sabrina and Roxanne peeked out of their cabin. They rushed forward to see what their sisters had found.

"Get away from the trunk!" Demetra warned, but it was too late.

The second the four princesses surrounded the trunk, all four of their jewels lit up.

"Oh, dear!" Sabrina cried, touching her head.

Now the little leather trunk began to glow.

"I think we found the crown!" Emily

gasped as she struggled to hold onto the trunk.

"No kidding!" Roxanne cried.

"What's all that noise?" Rudgrin stuck her head down below. One look at the four princesses with their glowing jewels and she screeched, "Guards! Come quickly!"

"What do we do now?" Emily cried.

"Split up!" Demetra announced.

"No!" Roxanne ordered. "Hold my hand!"

Demetra shot Roxanne an irritated look. "Roxanne, this is no time to argue."

"Right!" Roxanne said through clenched teeth. "Now, do as I say."

The Ruby Princess raised her magic shield. It had the power to make her invisible. Roxanne gripped Demetra's hand. Then Sabrina and Emily put their hands on Roxanne's shoulder as the

Darkling guards appeared at the top of the ladder. Then Princess Roxanne chanted:

"Magic shield, so strong and true,
Make us disappear from view!"

"Seize them!" Rudgrin wailed. The Darklings dove down the ladder and froze.

"Seize who?" one of the Darklings asked. "There's no one here."

Escape from the *Sea Shadow*

The Jewel Princesses were invisible, but they didn't dare move or breathe. Darklings were all around them.

The girls stood like statues staring at the ladder. It was their only way out, and the Darkling captain was blocking it. They had to distract him.

Princess Emily remembered she had a rope under her cape. It was from one of the black bags she had found.

She raised the rope in the air. It looked like it was floating by itself. Emily shook the rope in front of a Darkling's face.

"Help!" the Darkling cried.

"Get back!" the captain barked. "There is a curse on this boat."

Emily wiggled the rope in front of the captain's face. "*Whoo!*" she moaned.

"*Yargh!*" The captain leaped away from the ladder. He huddled against the wall with his Darkling crew. "Don't go near that," he ordered.

This was it — the Jewel Princesses' chance to escape. But they had to move fast. They carried the trunk up the ladder. At the top, Emily threw the rope at the Darklings.

"Look out!" the Darklings shrieked, covering their hooded faces. "The curse!"

Once they were on deck, the Jewel Princesses let go of one another's hands. They were no longer invisible, but they didn't care. They hurried to find a way off the ship.

Sabrina pointed to a rowboat. "Let's put the crown in it and make our getaway," she whispered.

The princesses swung the rowboat over the side of the ship and climbed in.

"Emily!" Roxanne called from inside the boat. "Let's go!"

"I'm coming. I just have to get one thing." Emily was still angry about the banners stolen from her kingdom. She raced to grab the box of banners.

"Hurry, Emily!" Demetra hissed, "before one of the Darklings sees you!"

Emily loaded the banner box into the

rowboat. Then, for good measure, she dropped two heavy bags and another box in with it.

"Stop it this instant!" Sabrina ordered. "This little boat isn't big enough for all of those bags and boxes."

Emily ignored Sabrina and hopped into the boat.

The princesses used the rope pulleys to lower themselves into the Black Sea. The green fog was so thick they could hardly see the water.

Sabrina wrinkled her nose. "This water smells."

"Like rotten eggs," Emily agreed.

"Let's get out of here before someone sees us," Princess Demetra said, looking back at the ship. "Everyone grab an oar and row."

Roxanne's stomach felt much better now. She grabbed an oar and rowed with all her might.

"Where do we go?" Demetra squinted into the fog. "I can't see a thing."

"That way!" Sabrina pointed one way and Emily the other.

"Well, make up your minds," Roxanne huffed. "We can't go both ways."

"This is hard," Sabrina murmured. "If we make the right choice, we'll row ourselves back to the Jewel Kingdom."

"If we make the wrong choice," Demetra said, "we'll row to the other side of the Black Sea."

"Where Lord Bleak is," Roxanne added.

Sabrina shivered. "Let's not make the wrong choice."

"All right," Princess Emily said boldly. "Then let's go my way."

The others looked at her doubtfully.

"If you're sure . . ." Roxanne began.

The Emerald Princess nodded her head. "I'm sure. My way will take us home."

"All right," Demetra said firmly. The princesses ducked their heads and rowed as hard as they could away from the *Sea Shadow*.

But with each stroke of their oars, the boat sank lower and lower in the water.

"We're sinking!" Sabrina cried, as more and more of the Black Sea splashed into their boat. "The rowboat must have a leak."

"There's no leak," Demetra replied. "It's Emily's boxes and bags."

"Then toss them overboard!" Roxanne cried.

"Oh, no, you don't!" Emily threw herself across the box with the banners. "This was stolen from my land, and I'm taking it home."

"We'll never get home if you keep this up," Demetra snapped.

"Stop fighting, and start helping!" Sabrina cried. She scooped up handfuls of water and tossed them over the side of their boat.

"We're going down!" Roxanne declared as she bailed water into the Black Sea with her shield.

Just then the fog cleared. There, directly in front of them, lay a tiny cove. Its beach was bordered with large boulders.

"Land!" Sabrina whispered.

The soggy rowboat ran aground with a crunch in the shallow water. The girls grabbed the trunk containing the Great

Jeweled Crown, leaped out of the boat, and waded the rest of the way to shore.

"We made it!" Roxanne cried, wrapping her arms around her sisters. "We made it!"

Thunder crashed, and lightning lit up the beach.

A tall figure in a hooded cape stood in front of a gigantic rock fortress.

"Welcome, Princesses," he said in a chilling voice. "So glad you could make it to my home."

Lord Bleak

"Lord Bleak!" Princess Roxanne gasped. "It's you!"

The caped figure slowly turned his head. For the first time in their lives, the princesses saw the face of Lord Bleak. His skin was covered with boils. His eyes glowed like burning coals. His mouth twisted into a smile that showed black, broken teeth.

"Yes, it is I," Lord Bleak hissed. "Now,

be good little girls, and give me that crown."

"No!" Roxanne shouted. "You can never have this crown. Ever!"

Lord Bleak's lip curled into a sneer. "As you wish."

He snapped his fingers, and giant spiders appeared from behind every rock. Their furry black legs wriggled beneath their shiny round bodies. They snapped their jaws like sharp scissors.

Demetra nearly fainted. "Spiders," she gasped. "I hate spiders."

Sabrina caught hold of Demetra's arm. "Don't think of them as spiders," she whispered. "Think of them as big ugly bugs."

"I'm trying," Demetra said as the spiders crawled closer and closer. "But it isn't helping."

The princesses clung to one another and backed down the beach.

"As soon as we hit the water," Roxanne whispered, "run for the rowboat."

"Couldn't we run sooner than that?" Emily squeaked.

But it was too late. Long threads shot out from the spiders and coiled around the princesses.

"They're tying us up!" Sabrina cried as more threads looped around them.

The threads flew from every side. Within seconds the princesses were roped back-to-back at the center of a giant web.

The trunk with the Great Jeweled Crown lay on its side at their feet.

"Help!" Emily called to her sisters. "I'm caught."

"Me, too," Demetra said, trying to move her arm.

A familiar voice giggled from the beach. It was Princess Rudgrin. She had anchored the *Sea Shadow* and taken another rowboat to shore.

"Poor little princesses," Rudgrin said. "They look pitiful. Don't they, Father?"

"I'll tell you who's pitiful," Roxanne said, struggling to get free. "You!"

Rudgrin snarled at Roxanne and opened the trunk. The Great Jeweled Crown lay inside. It was covered with jewels of every color. It was the most beautiful, magical crown in all the land.

Rudgrin carried the crown to her father and knelt. "Here is the Great Jeweled Crown, Father. Wear it well."

"At last!" Lord Bleak's eyes gleamed. "I have the power back."

He raised the crown above his head in triumph. But his smile quickly disappeared.

"Something is wrong!" Lord Bleak hissed. "It doesn't have the strength it once had."

He turned his burning red eyes on his daughter. "What have you done to it?"

Princess Rudgrin shrank away from him. "Nothing, Father," she whimpered. "I swear."

"You must have done something," he growled.

While Lord Bleak and his daughter argued, the princesses tried to break free of the web.

"If I could just get my elbow loose," Roxanne muttered, "maybe I could get free."

"It's no use," Demetra cried. "I can't budge."

"It does appear to be hopeless," Sabrina murmured.

"Don't give up," Emily whispered. "I can get us out of this if we just work together."

"What do we do?" Sabrina whispered back.

"Listen to me," the Emerald Princess replied, "and do exactly as I say."

Princess Emily's pan flute hung from a gold cord at her waist. She couldn't reach it, but Demetra could. Demetra passed the flute from her hand to Roxanne's elbow. Roxanne passed it from her elbow to Sabrina's shoulder. Sabrina turned and moved the flute in front of Emily's mouth.

"If I blow the high note on this flute," Emily explained, "we will shrink. If I blow the low note, we'll grow big. Which should it be?"

There was no question about it.

"Big!" the other princesses chorused.

Emily took a deep breath and blew the lowest note.

The thick webbing snapped with a loud *twang*!

Lord Bleak and Princess Rudgrin heard the noise and spun around. They watched the princesses grow as tall as trees.

"They're giants!" Rudgrin gasped.

"That's right, Rudgrin," Princess Roxanne boomed. "And we giants want our crown back."

Rudgrin dove behind the nearest boulder. The giant spiders ran for the castle.

Bleak tried to cover the crown under his cape, but it was glowing. He couldn't hide it!

Emily took a giant step forward. "Hand over the crown, Bleak!" she ordered.

The closer Princess Emily got to the Great Jeweled Crown, the more her jewel began to shine.

Lord Bleak jerked away from her, shielding his eyes with one hand.

"Do you see what's happening?" Princess Sabrina whispered to Demetra. "Emily's light is blinding him."

"Then what are we waiting for?" Princess Demetra cried. "Let's get him!"

"Hold hands!" Princess Roxanne called as they formed a circle around Lord Bleak. "Let's use all of our jewel power."

Lord Bleak screamed as the glow from the jewels grew stronger and stronger.

"Get away from me!" he howled. "The crown is mine."

"It will never be yours!" the princesses cried. Together, their jewels made a dazzling rainbow.

"Look!" Princess Sabrina called as the rainbow swirled around Lord Bleak. "Our light is destroying his darkness!"

Lord Bleak sank to his knees. "Stop!"

"Oh, Great Jeweled Crown, show us your light," Princess Emily chanted.

"Bring back the day," Princess Roxanne added.

"And stop the Bleak night," Princess Demetra said.

As each princess spoke, Lord Bleak grew smaller and smaller.

And when Princess Sabrina said, *"Long may the light shine in our Jewel Kingdom!"* he vanished. And so did the castle, the spiders, and Princess Rudgrin.

A heap of black cloth was all that remained of the evil Lord Bleak.

And next to the cloth shone the Great Jeweled Crown.

Fly Away Home

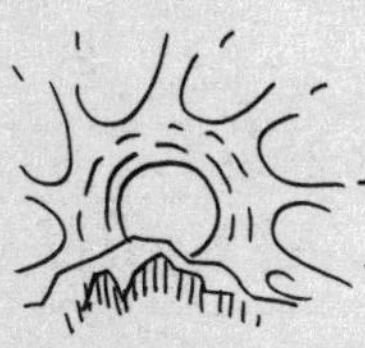

The Jewel Princesses had to wait until sundown to change back to their normal size. They stood on the empty beach, holding hands until the last ray of light from the sun disappeared.

Then the Sapphire Princess reached for her magic dust. It was in the small blue pouch she always wore at her waist.

"Are we ready to go home?" Princess Sabrina asked.

"More than ready," Princess Roxanne answered.

"We have the crown," Princess Emily said.

Princess Demetra pointed to the east. "And we know the way. Let's go."

The Sapphire Princess tossed her magic dust in the air and chanted:

"Up in the air and through the sky,
Home with the Jeweled Crown, let us fly!"

Suddenly they lifted off the ground and were floating through clouds. Before they knew it the Black Sea was far behind them.

There was a half moon that evening. A few stars twinkled in the sky.

"This is so peaceful," Princess Sabrina sighed. "It's hard to believe that only a while ago we were fighting our worst enemy."

"If Emily hadn't thought of blowing her pan flute, we would still be trapped in that awful spider's web," Demetra said with a shudder.

"I couldn't have done it alone," Emily replied. "I needed everyone's help to reach my flute."

Roxanne grinned. "It's amazing what can happen when we princesses work together."

The princesses crossed the Borderlands into the Jewel Kingdom. Below them they could see the Rushing River. Soon they were passing over Buttercup Meadow. The Jewel Palace gleamed in the distance.

"What are we going to tell Mother and

Father about all of this?" Emily asked as they drew closer to home.

"That's a good question," Sabrina replied. "If we tell them the whole truth, they'll be worried sick."

"And Twitter will get in trouble for letting someone break into the tower," Demetra pointed out.

"Why should we tell them anything?" Roxanne asked. "We have the Great Jeweled Crown back. No one was hurt. The kingdom is safe."

"Maybe we should keep this to ourselves for now," Emily said. "It will be our princess secret."

Roxanne, Demetra, and Sabrina nodded in agreement.

A princess secret.

About the Authors

JAHNNA N. MALCOLM stands for Jahnna "and" Malcolm. Jahnna Beecham and Malcolm Hillgartner are married and write together. They have written over seventy books for kids. Jahnna N. Malcolm have written about ballerinas, horses, ghosts, singing cowgirls, and green slime.

Before Jahnna and Malcolm wrote books, they were actors. They met on the stage where Malcolm was playing a prince. And they were married on the stage where Jahnna was playing a princess.

Now they have their own little prince and princess: Dash and Skye. They all live in Ashland, Oregon, with their big red dog, Ruby, and their fluffy little white dog, Clarence.

A World of Dazzling Magic
THE JEWEL KINGDOM